THE PARABLE OF THE PEACOCK II
THE SAGA CONTINUES

A Read-Aloud Picture Book for Thoughtful Citizens

Written by Brent Bohlen
Illustrated by Oksana Basarab

Salvage America Publications

Salvage America Publications
ISBN: 978-1-7335757-5-1

10 9 8 7 6 5 4 3 2 1

DEDICATION

The first Peacock book was dedicated to our nation's founders who gave us the constitutional right of free speech and to journalists who preserve that right by speaking truth to power. The ensuing year proves they deserve that recognition once again.

ACKNOWLEDGMENTS

I acknowledge for the second time the incomparable contributions of jack-of-all-trades publisher Jeff Salvage, extraordinary artist Oksana Basarab and editor and supportive wife, Mary. But I also thank the many citizens who have voiced their appreciation of the first book and encouraged me to continue producing memes until enough material existed for a second. Of course, neither book would have been possible without the vast array of material supplied by the Peacock himself. I acknowledge, but do not thank him, because without his contributions this cathartic venture would have been unnecessary.

A warning to pig-sheep out on the limb
Peacock's fall guys will be anyone but him.
The horses are trying to prune that branch
But their odds are not worth betting the ranch.
Meanwhile Weasel is going to town
Doing his best to bring everything down.

11/26/19

A pitbull went after organized crime
And sent many thugs away to do time.
It launched him as a political player
Who then became a big city mayor.
After 9/11 the pitbull shined.
It's too bad that since then he's lost his mind.
He works to help Peacock create illusions
Tilting at windmills that are delusions.
The raging dog has, to this reporter,
Changed the meaning of "rabid supporter."

12/13/19

Turtle thinks no House bill is a keeper
And takes pride in his name, "The Grim Reaper."
Even bipartisan bills come to die,
Giving ALL voters a poke in the eye.
Now he wants an act of prostitution
Of Senate duty to the Constitution.

1/16/20

One side is led by a prideful peacock
Who has mesmerized his abiding flock.
His sheep willingly forgive every sin
Committed by Peacock and all his kin.
The other side, though, looks up to a swan
Who leads with mindful grace from dawn to dawn.
While Peacock rages and lies hour by hour,
Swan with calm resolve speaks the truth to power.

1/30/20

"Heads on a pike" was metaphorical,
But the threat was more than rhetorical.
The Senate pig-sheep were scared through and through –
Don't need Profiles in Courage – Volume Two.
The cowards caved – abandoned all of us –
Threw the Constitution under the bus.
Rigging elections has a nasty ring,
But facts don't matter when you have a king.
Everyone knows what this monarch is like,
Four more years and REAL heads are on a pike.

Corruptive Influences on American Democracy

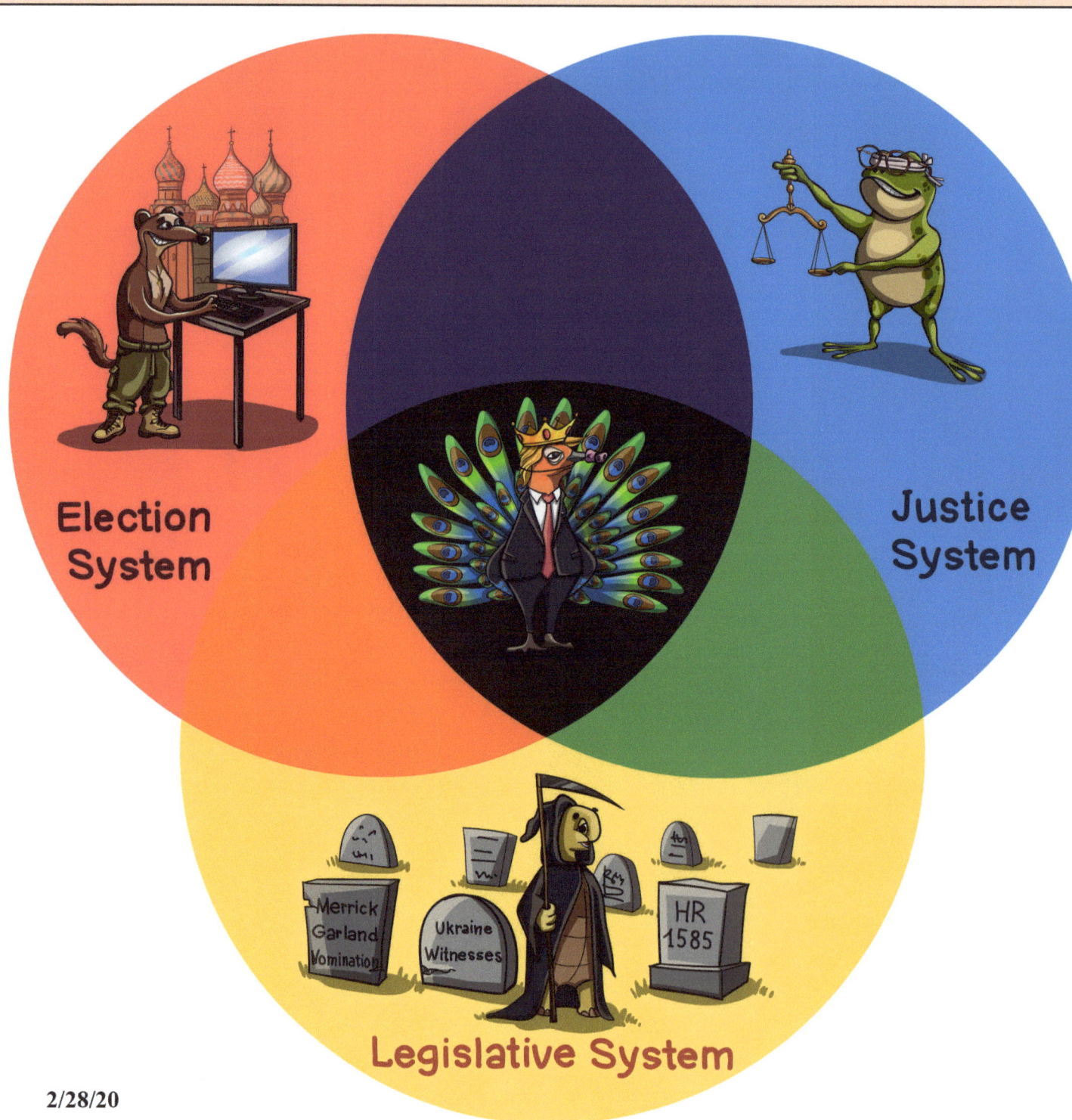

Election System

Justice System

Legislative System

2/28/20

Now everyone understands more fully
That Peacock's fearful like any bully.
It looked weak when the bird bunkered to hide.
Optics are better when boldly outside.
But a throng had gathered out there, you see,
Until dispersed by his toady A.G.
Then Peacock and his low band of jesters
Would not even face peaceful protesters.
A leader guides us to a better place,
But we got a photo op to save face.

6/6/20

The peacock's had a bad couple of weeks –
Not been the kind of press that a campaign seeks:
Several setbacks in the Supreme Court,
A botched go at the SDNY fort,
The rally that fizzled in Tulsa town,
Covid's sharp rise led to reshutting down,
A "White Power" tweet was a big to-do,
Russian bounties showed he's without a clue.
Peacock's poll numbers are really draggin.'
It looks like the wheels are off his wagon.

'PEACOCK'S RE-ELECTION BANDWAGON'

Looks like the wheels are coming off.

7/5/20

Peacock, toady A.G. and motley crew
Stir another toxic Friday-night brew.
U.S. Attorneys keep meeting their ends
For looking into Peacock and his friends.
Now a Stone-cold felon won't serve penance
Because the bird commuted his sentence.
They must think we are just dumber than stumps
To not see through all their weekend news dumps.

This intergalactic alien sleuth
Patrols the cosmos in support of truth.
Twenty thousand false and misleading claims
Put Peacock on the List of Liars' Names.

7/20/20

Peacock needs distractions from Covid fails
Ere his campaign goes further off the rails.
The bird and toad A.G. hope to provoke
Protestors who are in the street and woke.
Sans secret police, no tyrant is whole,
And with them a nation loses its soul.
Gestapo, Stasi, KGB, Savak –
Fowl's secret police are chips off the block.
Each unnamed storm trooper and unmarked van
Brings freedom closer to the garbage can.

Although Dr. GOAT is long in the tooth,
In Covid time he's Giver Of All Truth.
He offered sage advice on the virus,
But where was our leader to inspire us?
For months Peacock failed at this basic task
By not convincing all to wear a mask.
And now our Covid death toll keeps mounting
One hundred sixty thousand and counting.

Peacock's world is his imagination,
And it's become the bane of our nation.
He cannot see things from our perspective.
His personality is defective.
Another four years — it really matters —
Would leave our country torn and in tatters.

When the animals look to place the blame,
They will find the culprit who fed the flame.
Peacock worked to get his sheep really turnt,
And now our democracy's getting burnt.

9/5/20

Peacock can't understand a selfless act.
Empathy is a trait he's always lacked.
You see our fallen soldiers as heroes,
While the prideful fowl views them as zeroes.
He dissed the Gold-Star Khans and John McCain.
Peacock is unable to feel your pain.
"Suckers" and "Losers" – He denies each word.
But who would believe this big lying bird?

Commander-in-Chief "Bone Spurs" Peacock Addresses the Troops:

Suckers!
Losers!

9/9/20

"Fake News!" Peacock charges. We roll our eyes.
He's the one who told twenty thousand lies.
Peacock claims his foe is mentally dense,
But it's the bird who talks and makes no sense.
Fowl claims his foe is starting to dodder,
But then there's bird's ramp and glass of water.
Peacock faults others for his behavior.
That's no leader who could be our savior.

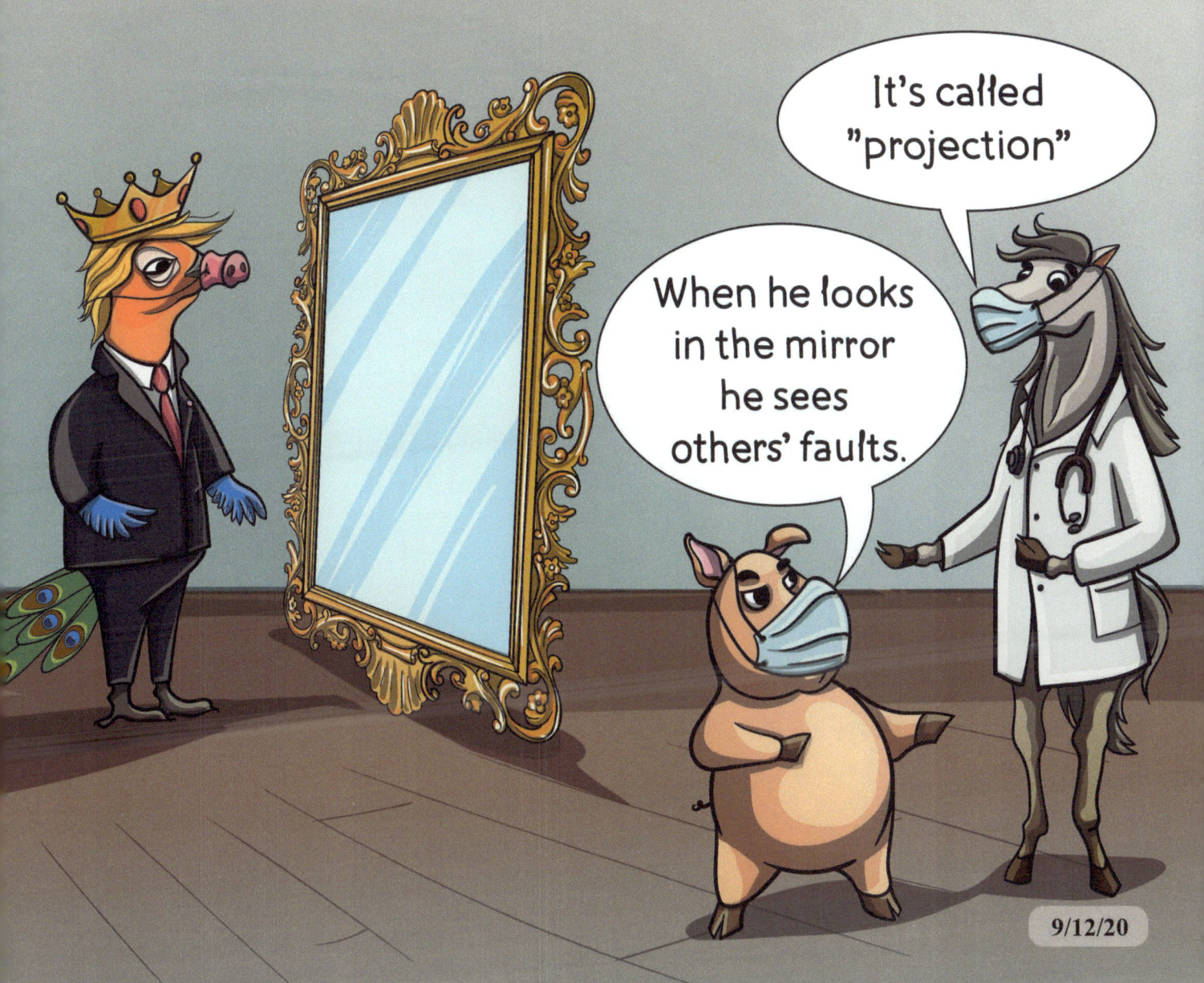

When things are totaled on the leader board
Peacock's a leader we cannot afford.
Elect him again? No! We do not dare.
That's a burden our country cannot bear.

Turtle's out of his shell for all to see
The naked truth of his hypocrisy.
His old principle of when to do what
Turns out to have meant nothing but squat.
It's the new leader who should have the key
To replace Notorious RBG.
So we call him out with "Liar, Liar …
If Turtle had on pants, they'd be on fire."

As soon as you want, Sire.

9/23/20

The election is nigh – a campaign of note.
We hope they will count every last vote.
Then we will find out how much is yet to run.
Is our nightmare over – or just begun?
Here are four roads to the future ahead.
Two could lead to our democracy dead.

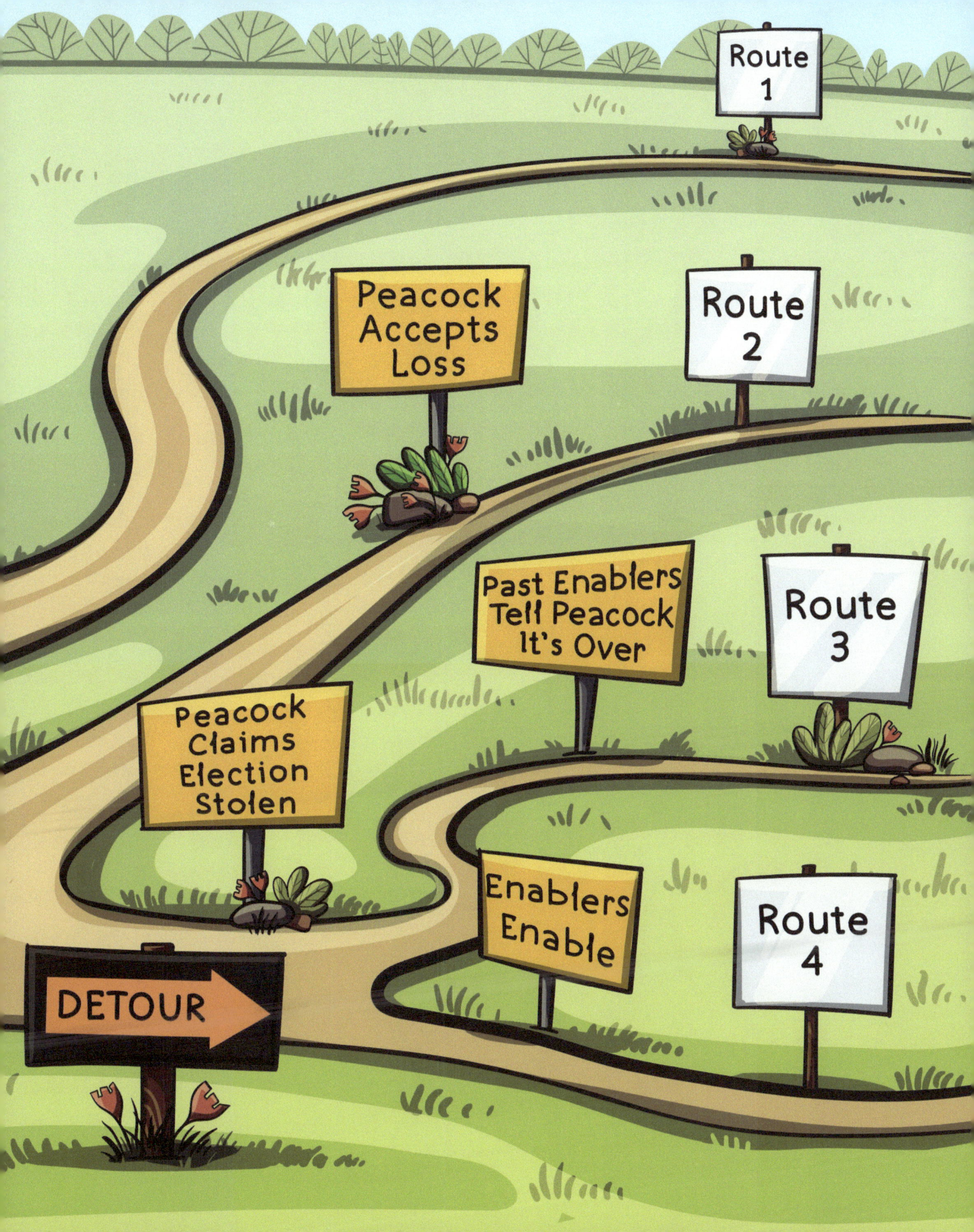

The Day After The Votes Are Counted
(or, perhaps, after the Supreme Court rules)

Not being a winner left Peacock peeved,
And yet somehow he felt a bit relieved.
He'll no longer have to deal with "Fake News."
Peacock will listen to just his own views.

The Day After The Votes Are Counted
(or, perhaps, after the Supreme Court rules)

Route 4

Peacock wants his tyranny to flower.
The sky's his limit to stay in power.
His enablers will gladly join the fray
Or at least hide and keep out of the way.
We pray his followers won't take up arms
As that would leave our land with untold harms.

About the Author

Brent Bohlen of Springfield, Illnois, retired from a career in and around state and local government that included being a prosecutor, legal counsel for a taxpayer group and a commissioner on a state public utilities commission. He also authored BoomerWalk, which encourages baby boomers to take up Olympic-style race walking as a highly aerobic, low-impact form of exercise.

About the Illustrator

Oksana Basarab lives and works in Lviv, Ukraine, using Illustrator, Photoshop and sometimes real tools for creativity. She specializes in children's cartoon illustrations. Her portfolio includes more than a dozen books and manuals and countless illustrations for posters, leaflets, patterns, web applications and other products.

About the Publisher

Jeff Salvage of Medford, New Jersey, owner of Salvage America Publications, has published many books under various imprints. He teaches computer science at Drexel University, is an accomplished photographer and was an international athlete.

Website

Please visit *www.peacockparable.com* to shop for merchandise related to **The Parable of the Peacock** and to sign up for our email list to stay in touch about future creations.